Grandpa I Just Wanna be a Cowboy:

Women in the West

Books by Trae Q.L. Venerable

Grandpa I Just Wanna be a Cowboy: Notables from the West
Grandpa I Just Wanna be a Cowboy: Rodeo Cowboys
Grandpa I Just Wanna be a Cowboy: Women in the West

Grandpa I Just Wanna be a Cowboy:

Women in the West

Trae Q.L. Venerable

SPEAKING VOLUMES, LLC
NAPLES, FLORIDA
2020

Grandpa I Just Wanna be a Cowboy:
Women in the West

ISBN 978-1-62815-715-4

History has defined us for a long time.
But now, the truth about the
forgotten cowboys will come to the
light.

For all of the forgotten cowboys...
- Trae Q. L. Venerable

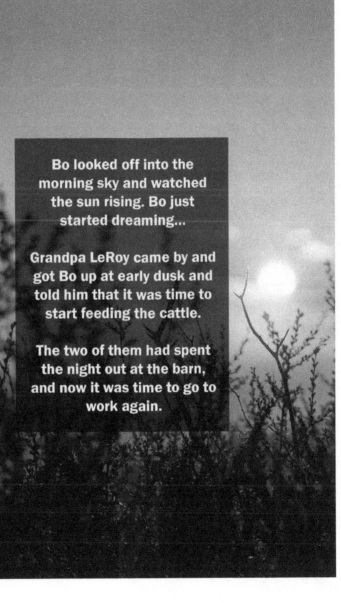

Bo looked off into the morning sky and watched the sun rising. Bo just started dreaming...

Grandpa LeRoy came by and got Bo up at early dusk and told him that it was time to start feeding the cattle.

The two of them had spent the night out at the barn, and now it was time to go to work again.

While Grandpa was getting the bales of hay, Bo was thinking about everything he had learned about people who helped shape the west, and rodeo cowboys so far.

When Grandpa came back, Bo asked, "Grandpa LeRoy I have a question?"

Grandpa replied, "Shoot it at me."

Bo went on, "It's cool that there were black cowboys but were there black women in the wild west?"

Grandpa smiled and then replied, "You have no idea!"

He yelled out at the top of his lungs to his Grandpa,

"I wanna be a cowboy"

"I wanna be a cowboy"

"I just wanna be a cowboy"

Grandpa replied, "Just as you want to be a black cowboy, the women wanted to be cowgirls just as bad."

"Bo, just as the black cowboys wanted respect so did the black Women in the West. Women just wanted a little respect and it was hard to come by."

Grandpa explained, "The first Woman in the West was Biddy Mason. She was one for the ages. Mason was a Californian real-estate entrepreneur and philanthropist. In 1872, Mason was a founding member of the First African Methodist Episcopal Church... the city's first black church."

Grandpa added, "She had to work hard for everything she had in her life!"

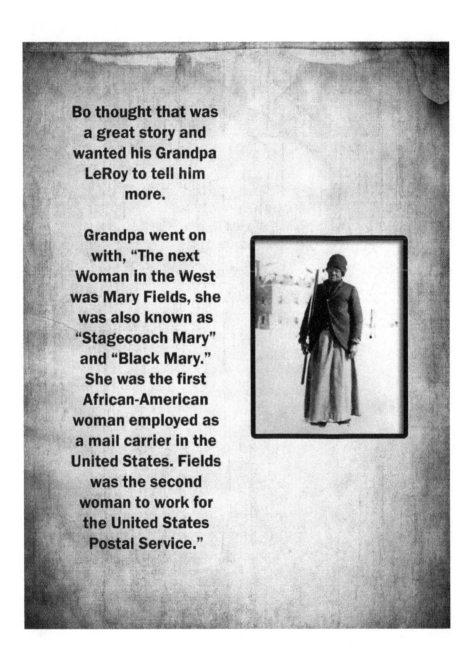

Bo thought that was a great story and wanted his Grandpa LeRoy to tell him more.

Grandpa went on with, "The next Woman in the West was Mary Fields, she was also known as "Stagecoach Mary" and "Black Mary." She was the first African-American woman employed as a mail carrier in the United States. Fields was the second woman to work for the United States Postal Service."

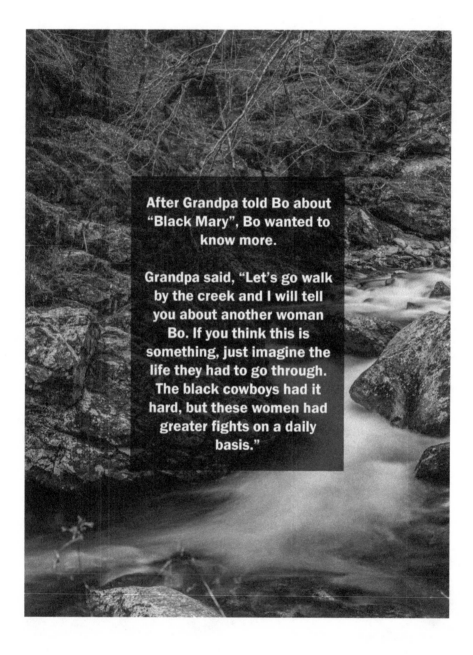

After Grandpa told Bo about "Black Mary", Bo wanted to know more.

Grandpa said, "Let's go walk by the creek and I will tell you about another woman Bo. If you think this is something, just imagine the life they had to go through. The black cowboys had it hard, but these women had greater fights on a daily basis."

As they were walking...

Grandpa discussed the next Woman in the West. "Her name was Cathay Williams and she was very special because she was the only woman to serve in the U.S. Army as a Buffalo Soldier. She enlisted as a man in 1866 and tricked the U.S. Army so she could fight for her country. Bo, these times were rough in general, women weren't allowed to serve in the military.

Grandpa added, "She had the guts to follow her dreams no matter what. More guts than people have today." Bo thought that Cathay was just the coolest for doing what she did.

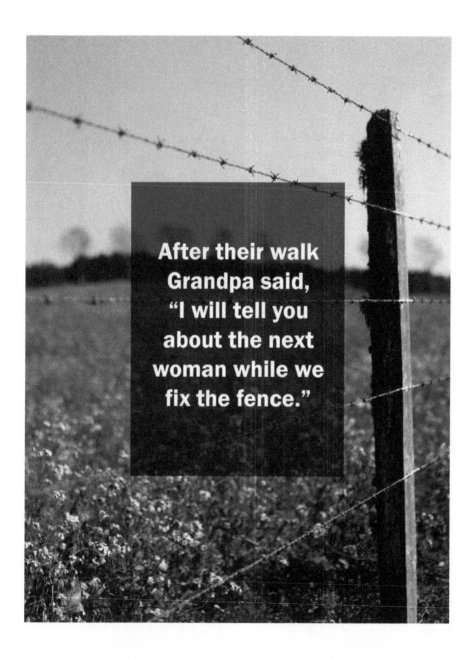

After their walk
Grandpa said,
"I will tell you
about the next
woman while we
fix the fence."

As they were fixing the fence...

Grandpa said to Bo, "Mary Pleasant, she was a 19th-Century African American entrepreneur widely known as Mammy Pleasant. She used her wealth to help end slavery and worked hard on the Underground Railroad. Also, in the 1880s as a result of her actions she was called "The Mother of Human Rights in California."

Bo was exhausted after fixing the fence but surely needed to know more.

Bo and Grandpa went to the truck to get their medical supplies.

Now they were ready to doctor any animal that needed it.

Grandpa said, "I will tell you about the next Woman in the West, as we go check on the cattle in the pastures. Hop in the truck."

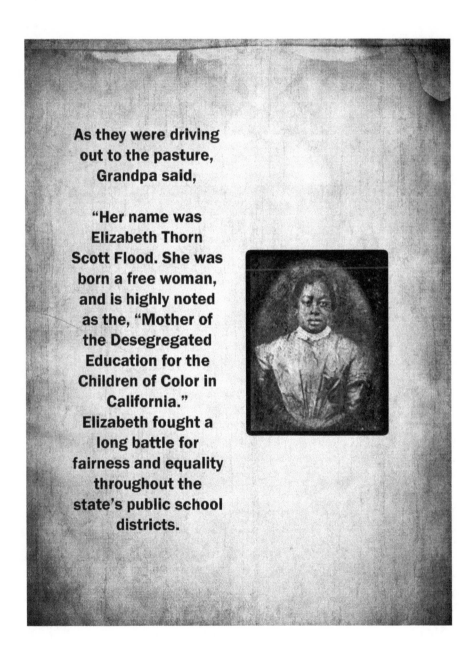

As they were driving out to the pasture, Grandpa said,

"Her name was Elizabeth Thorn Scott Flood. She was born a free woman, and is highly noted as the, "Mother of the Desegregated Education for the Children of Color in California." Elizabeth fought a long battle for fairness and equality throughout the state's public school districts.

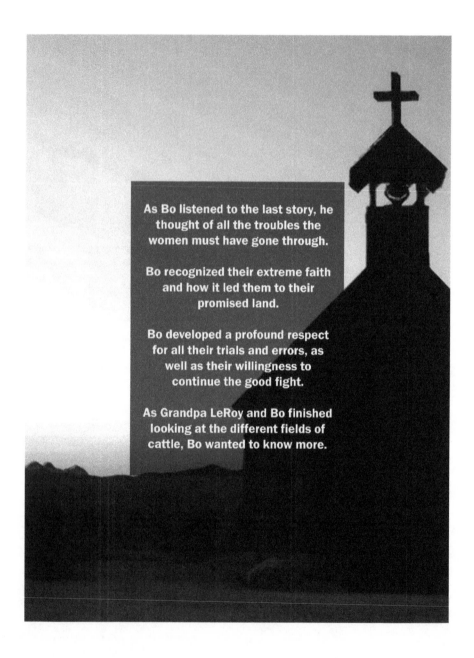

As Bo listened to the last story, he thought of all the troubles the women must have gone through.

Bo recognized their extreme faith and how it led them to their promised land.

Bo developed a profound respect for all their trials and errors, as well as their willingness to continue the good fight.

As Grandpa LeRoy and Bo finished looking at the different fields of cattle, Bo wanted to know more.

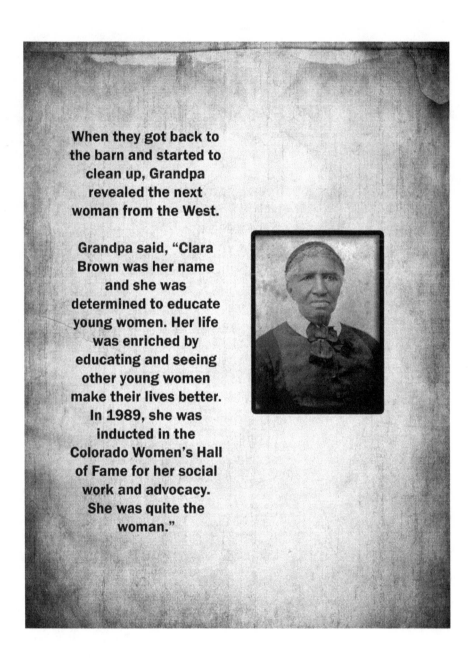

When they got back to the barn and started to clean up, Grandpa revealed the next woman from the West.

Grandpa said, "Clara Brown was her name and she was determined to educate young women. Her life was enriched by educating and seeing other young women make their lives better. In 1989, she was inducted in the Colorado Women's Hall of Fame for her social work and advocacy. She was quite the woman."

After all their work was done, the cows were happy, and Bo's head was full of the Women in the West, Bo and Grandpa headed home.

Grandpa LeRoy said, "Let's go back home, there is more to learn when we get back!"

Bo replied, "Gee Grandpa, I can't wait."

The two of them set off for home.

When they got home,
Bo was still in shock
with all he had learned
today.

He took a second and
imagined what it was
like in the Wild West!

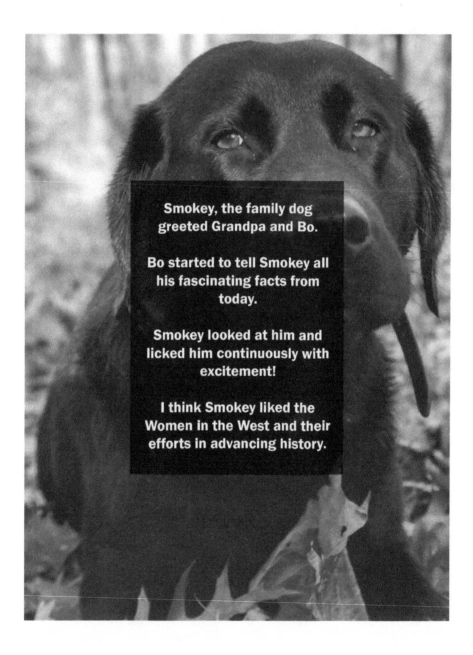

Smokey, the family dog greeted Grandpa and Bo.

Bo started to tell Smokey all his fascinating facts from today.

Smokey looked at him and licked him continuously with excitement!

I think Smokey liked the Women in the West and their efforts in advancing history.

Once Bo finished telling his wonders to Smokey, Grandpa came to get Bo and they went to do a few more chores at the house before he took Bo on a surprise trip!

First, they needed to feed and give water to their other hunting dogs. Next, Grandpa LeRoy was going to tell Bo about another fascinating Woman in the West.

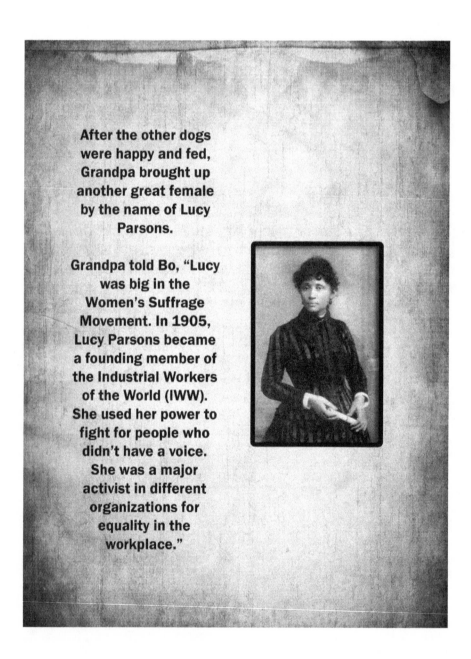

After the other dogs were happy and fed, Grandpa brought up another great female by the name of Lucy Parsons.

Grandpa told Bo, "Lucy was big in the Women's Suffrage Movement. In 1905, Lucy Parsons became a founding member of the Industrial Workers of the World (IWW). She used her power to fight for people who didn't have a voice. She was a major activist in different organizations for equality in the workplace."

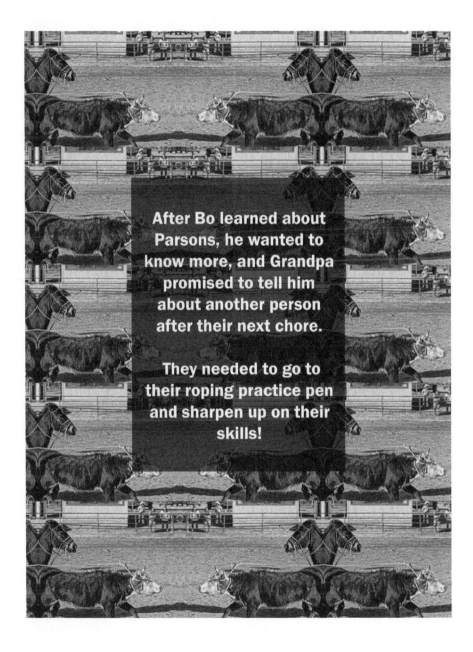

After Bo learned about Parsons, he wanted to know more, and Grandpa promised to tell him about another person after their next chore.

They needed to go to their roping practice pen and sharpen up on their skills!

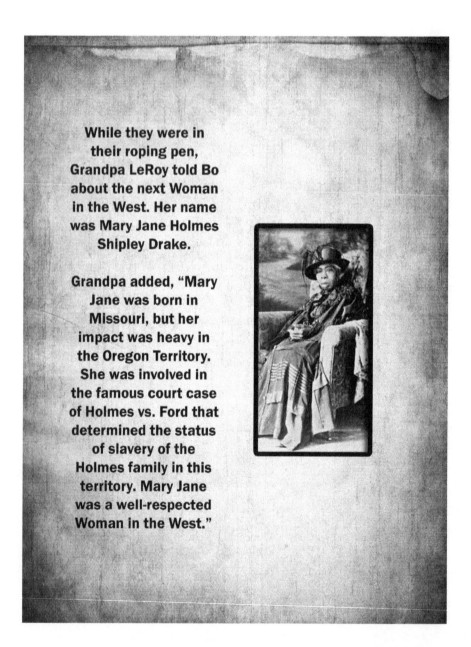

While they were in their roping pen, Grandpa LeRoy told Bo about the next Woman in the West. Her name was Mary Jane Holmes Shipley Drake.

Grandpa added, "Mary Jane was born in Missouri, but her impact was heavy in the Oregon Territory. She was involved in the famous court case of Holmes vs. Ford that determined the status of slavery of the Holmes family in this territory. Mary Jane was a well-respected Woman in the West."

After hearing about Mary Jane, Bo and Grandpa finished their practice, and proceeded to put up their horses.

When they were done, Grandpa told Bo he was going to tell him about a couple of more Women in the West, and a surprise he had for him!

Bo and Grandpa LeRoy were almost finished with the chores.

One of the last chores was to help pick some walnuts off the walnut tree, so Grandma Julia Ann could make homemade Black Walnut Ice Cream.

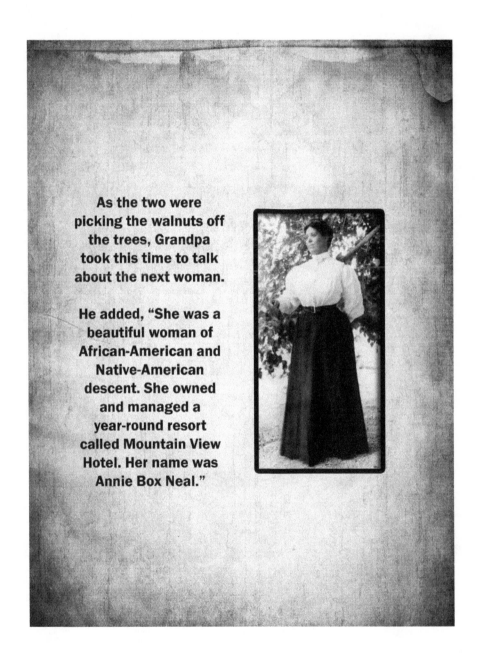

As the two were picking the walnuts off the trees, Grandpa took this time to talk about the next woman.

He added, "She was a beautiful woman of African-American and Native-American descent. She owned and managed a year-round resort called Mountain View Hotel. Her name was Annie Box Neal."

As Bo heard about Annie Box Neal, he was putting his picked walnuts in the basket.

He thought to himself how lucky he was to have the life he had and knew never to take anything for granted.

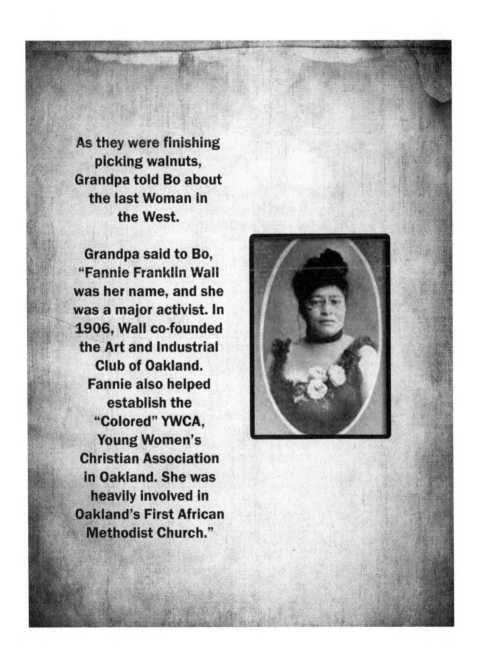

As they were finishing picking walnuts, Grandpa told Bo about the last Woman in the West.

Grandpa said to Bo, "Fannie Franklin Wall was her name, and she was a major activist. In 1906, Wall co-founded the Art and Industrial Club of Oakland. Fannie also helped establish the "Colored" YWCA, Young Women's Christian Association in Oakland. She was heavily involved in Oakland's First African Methodist Church."

When Bo heard about the last woman he was again beside himself. He felt so honored to hear these great Women in the West stories.

Grandpa and Bo brought the walnuts to the kitchen for Grandma Julia Ann to start making homemade ice cream.

Grandpa LeRoy and Bo couldn't wait because they knew it was going to be delicious.

After they had some ice cream, Bo wanted to know what the surprise was and Grandpa said, "You're in for a treat!"

Grandpa added, "Go get in the truck we are going into town!"

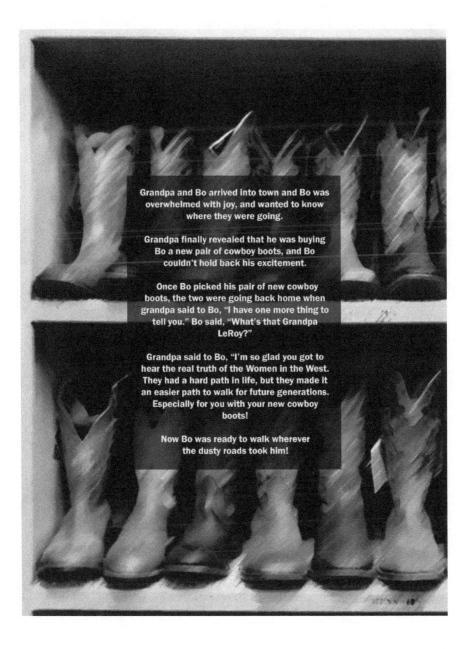

Grandpa and Bo arrived into town and Bo was overwhelmed with joy, and wanted to know where they were going.

Grandpa finally revealed that he was buying Bo a new pair of cowboy boots, and Bo couldn't hold back his excitement.

Once Bo picked his pair of new cowboy boots, the two were going back home when grandpa said to Bo, "I have one more thing to tell you." Bo said, "What's that Grandpa LeRoy?"

Grandpa said to Bo, "I'm so glad you got to hear the real truth of the Women in the West. They had a hard path in life, but they made it an easier path to walk for future generations. Especially for you with your new cowboy boots!

Now Bo was ready to walk wherever the dusty roads took him!

Author Bio

Trae Q.L Venerable, born to Myron and Tracy
Venerable with a life long history in
ranching and farming, is excited to bring
you *Grandpa I Just Wanna be a Cowboy*,
books of the "forgotten cowboys" history.
Trae, an avid outdoorsman, horseman and
cattle jock, comes from generations of
Farm and Ranch owners, from which many
of these stories have been passed on. For
way too long, the "forgotten cowboy" has
not been heard and the time is now.

Visit his website at:
www.traevenerable.com

On Sale Now!

For more information
visit: www.SpeakingVolumes.us

On Sale Now!

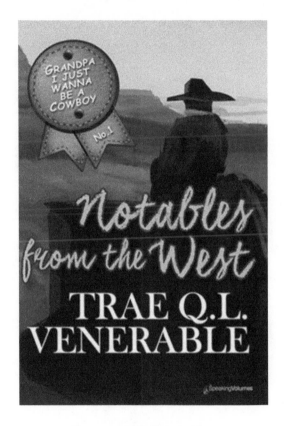

For more information
visit: www.SpeakingVolumes.us

CPSIA information can be obtained
at www.ICGtesting.com
Printed in the USA
LVHW032054140221
679286LV00003B/765

9 781628 157154